THE SUPER NERDS AND THE SNAIL ARMY OF DOOM

James Warwood

THE SUPER NERDS
AND THE SNAIL ARMY OF DOOM

Paperback ISBN: 978-1-915646-47-7
Ebook ASIN: 978-1-915646-48-4

Cover art & Interior design by James Warwood

www.cjwarwood.com

Give feedback on the book at:
me@cjwarwood.com

for all the nerds,

(myself included)

HI THERE,
i HOPE YOU ENJOY
THE BOOK

CHAPTER ONE
SNAILS

Here are three things you need to know before reading this book:

PURE EVIL

1. Snails are evil.

2. In every school there are always three blocked toilets, two nerds, and one weird caretaker.

3. Authors are good with words, but can't count.

4. And thirdly, superheroes are real.

Churchill Junior School is no different from your school. There are three blocked toilets, as well as five broken taps, one empty fish tank, and several very dry goldfish. There are two nerds who you will get to meet soon. And there is one weird caretaker, who could well be the most villainous supervillain the world has ever seen.

He is called **MR NITWHITT.**

THE SCHOOL CARETAKER

MAYBE A SUPER VILLAIN???

MAYBE JUST A BIT OF A WIERDO???

There are many rumours about the strange caretaker. Here are the best ones:

- He only eats egg mayo sandwiches, but with no mayo and no bread, so he really only eats mushed up boiled eggs.

- He collects snails, but nobody knows why.

- He is the evil twin of the Hunchback of Notre Dame, but the nation of France threw him out for being too smelly (and that's saying something because the nation of France is known for being the smelliest

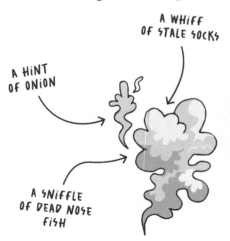

A WHIFF
OF STALE SOCKS

A HINT
OF ONION

A SNIFFLE
OF DEAD NOSE
FISH

people on the planet).

- He once picked his nose and pulled out a fish, but whether the fish was dead or alive is a subject of much debate in the playground.

- His favourite colour is dirt, which also happens to be his favourite shampoo.

- He HATES children, but enjoys seeing them suffer, which is why being a caretaker at a school is the perfect job for him.

THE LEGEND OF THE
DEAD NOSE FISH

There are also two nerds at Churchill Junior School, and I think you should meet them as well.

REGGIE loves maths.

MATHS GENIUS

ENGINEERING WHIZZ-KID

NERDY & PROUD

I ♡ PHYSICS

BEST FRIENDS WITH HILDA

I know, but just try to brush past that and you'll find he is also funny and loyal and an all-around nice guy.

He can actually do mental maths. I'm talking both crazy long algebraic equations and really hard sums in your head without a calculator. In his spare time, he doesn't watch cartoons or play video games or kick a football in the park. Reggie takes things apart and puts them back together again.

He has a tool belt he wears all the time, even while he sleeps. Hammer, screwdriver, monkey wrench, spirit level, duct tape, power drill, that bleepy thing that tells you if an electrical wire in a wall. The tool belt

LOCK PICKING TOOLS

THAT THING THAT NO ONE KNOWS WHAT iT DOES (EXCEPT REGGIE)

STANLY KNIFE

HAMMER

even has a pocket for an emergency sandwich (if you are wondering, today's choice was tuna and sweetcorn).

HILDA loves English.

GRAMMAR GODDESS

KNOW-IT-ALL

GEEKY & PROUD

BEST FRIENDS WITH REGGIE

I know, but just try to brush past that and you'll find she is also smart and caring and a wonderful human being.

She can actually read Shakespeare and understand it! Her idea of a good time is spotting a grammatical error in a textbook. For Hilda, finding a spelling error is like finding a fifty-pound note on the ground that also has the staff room's Wi-Fi password scribbled on the back.

You might assume that her backpack is full of perfectly polished homework. It actually contains a complete set of encyclopedias. Hilda takes all twelve hardbound books everywhere she goes. That way, if she doesn't understand something or can't answer a tricky question, she can look it up and learn something new. Because of this, her backpack weighs roughly the same as a mountain goat wearing all your mum's jewellery.

As for the existence of superheroes, well, this book is all the proof you'll need.

You see, this is the story of how the two *super nerds* of Churchill Junior School became the two school...

SUPER HEROES

CHAPTER TWO
PUDDLE

What a wonderful sound. It was the second best sound in the school day—the lunch bell. The only sound that tops it is, of course, the end of the school day bell.

The pupils of Churchill Junior School ran out of their classrooms as fast as cheetahs who had extra helpings of Weetabix for breakfast. Reggie and Hilda also ran, but not for the playground like everyone else. They were heading for their favourite bench at the front of the school to do what they always did at lunchtime.

AT WHAT EXACT LOCATION DID THE TITANIC SINK?

asked Reggie, as he fiddled with his dad's old VCR Machine in one hand and held his tuna and sweetcorn sandwich in the other.

Hilda reached into her backpack and picked out volume nine of her encyclopaedias. She thumbed through it until

MAYBE WE SHOULD AVOID THAT ICEBERG

NAH! THIS BOAT IS UNSINKABLE, RIGHT?

she reached the page she needed and took a bite of her chicken and stuffing sandwich. "Just as I thought. The Titanic sank on 14th April 1912 in the North Atlantic Ocean, three-hundred-and-seventy miles southeast of Newfoundland."

She adjusted her glasses and scanned down the page. "Did you also know that the ocean liner was described as *unsinkable* by the person who designed it but hit an iceberg on its maiden voyage? Because of the shipbuilder's arrogance, there were only twenty lifeboats aboard, which meant only a fraction of people survived."

"I love your follow-up facts, Hilda."

"Thanks, Reggie. So, what are you trying

to make today?"

Reggie took his last bite of sandwich and replied, "I'm not sure yet. My dad said it's a piece of old junk, but I reckon I can salvage some useful parts. What does VCR stand for?"

Hilda swapped her book for volume eleven and quickly found the entry. "Video Cassette Recorder. They revolutionised home television viewing in the 1980s. The machine could play videos by shining an infra-red LED light on magnetic tape, allowing viewers to pause and rewind a film and even record live TV."

Most kids would say *huh* as a large question mark would appear above their confused head. Not Reggie. He said, "Cool. I need an infra-red LED light for my home-

made night googles." As he set to work
extracting the precious component, another
question was directed at Hilda.

"Are super nerds allergic to fun?"

Hilda and Reggie looked up. It was a group
of kids from the class below them. Hilda
knew it was a stupid question, but one of
the character flaws of a know-it-all is that
they can never resist answering questions.
"Of course not," replied Hilda as she closed
volume eleven. "Fun is a subjective human
construct, not an organic matter. Therefore,
it is not possible to have an allergic reaction
to having fun."

Several question marks appeared. The
dominant kid stepped forward and
said, "how about this puddle?
Is that organic matter?"

"Yep."

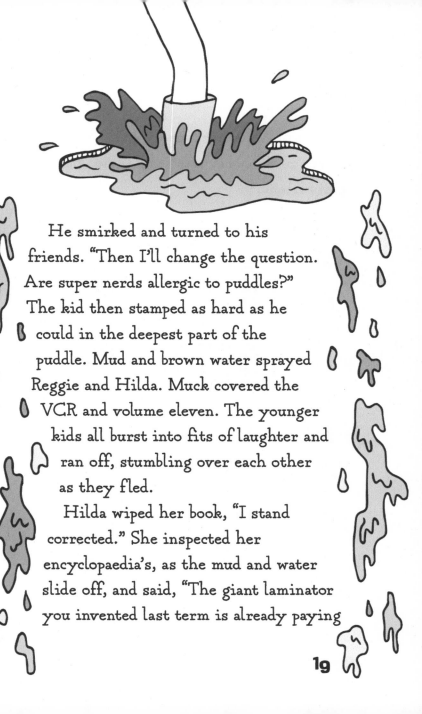

He smirked and turned to his friends. "Then I'll change the question. Are super nerds allergic to puddles?" The kid then stamped as hard as he could in the deepest part of the puddle. Mud and brown water sprayed Reggie and Hilda. Muck covered the VCR and volume eleven. The younger kids all burst into fits of laughter and ran off, stumbling over each other as they fled.

Hilda wiped her book, "I stand corrected." She inspected her encyclopaedia's, as the mud and water slide off, and said, "The giant laminator you invented last term is already paying for itself. Well done, super nerd!"

"You're welcome," replied Reggie, smiling at his friend.

Although the kids at school meant the name calling to be hurtful, the two best friends quite enjoyed being called *super nerds*. It set them apart from everyone else for being intelligent, which described them perfectly, and made them feel like they had superpowers.

As they wiped themselves down, a delivery driver skidded to a halt in front of the school gates. He leapt out of his van and ran up to Reggie and Hilda. "Could you too do me a favour and deliver this parcel to the school for me? I'm running a tad late."

Reggie read the name on the parcel. "It's addressed to the caretaker."

"I know," replied the delivery driver. "I try not to deliver his parcels in person if I can. There's a rumour at the depot that one delivery man went to deliver a parcel to Mr Nitwhitt, but they never returned. That was five years ago. No one has seen him since."

Reggie and Hilda looked at each other. They had reached the stage in their friendship where they didn't have to speak.

They could read each other's faces. Reggie's eyebrows were skyhigh. If they went any higher, they'd fly away and migrate for the winter. Hilda's skin tone turned even whiter than usually. Her eyeballs screamed the silent message. They agreed to refuse the parcel and never speak of this to anyone.

They turned to the delivery man, but the spot where he was standing was now occupied by a small, brown parcel. Then they looked at the van as it sped off at full speed as the delivery driver wound down the window and yelled, "Thanks, kids! I owe ya one."

CHAPTER THREE
PARCEL

Reggie picked up the parcel to take a closer look.

It was small. Roughly the size of a hamster giving another hamster a piggyback ride. The outside packaging was the usual boring brown. If you stare at the colour for too long, you start losing your hair and develop a keen interest in stamps. That's why postmen wear hats. But this parcel was different. It had an aurora.

"Hilda, do parcels normally glow?"

"Er," replied Hilda, wondering if it was worth consulting her encyclopaedia for this question. She decided to go it alone and said, "I suppose that would depend on the contains. Cleaning products and dishcloths, no. Radioactive material and glow sticks, yes."

"How about low-level humming and tiny vibrations?" Reggie sniffed. "And it smells of . . . hamsters?" He pulled a stanly knife from

his tool belt and was about to open it when Hilda shouted, "Stop! What do you think you're doing?"

"I was just going to take a little peek."

"But opening someone else's parcel is a criminal offence," said Hilda as she snatched the parcel out of his hands. "If you get thrown in jail, who will I spend lunchtime with?"

Reggie returned the knife into its allocated pouch and said,

UUUUM

"Aren't you a tiny bit curious to find out what's inside?"

"Of course I am," replied Hilda. "But I think you're forgetting whose name is on the parcel. The creep who sneezed on my head last week. And it was on purpose. He had a tissue in his other hand and still used my hair as a handkerchief."

Reggie added, "Don't forget when he cleaned the school fish tank with instant coffee and washing up liquid."

Hilda shivered. "I can still remember the smile on his face as he poured the whole fish tank down the toilet."

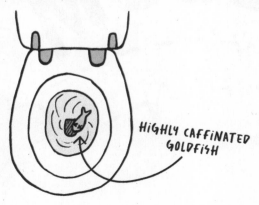

HIGHLY CAFFINATED GOLDFISH

"Plus, no one knows why he collects snails? For all we know, he could be creating an army of mutant snails to take over the school. We both know the caretaker is pure evil." Reggie pointed at the parcel and said, "What if this parcel contains something sinister? Something deadly he is planning to unleash in the school."

"Don't be ridiculous, Reggie." Hilda put the parcel on the bench and took a step back, just to be on the safe side. "Mr Nitwhitt is nasty, but pure evil is a step too far."

"Think about it. How many parcels have arrived for him in the past few weeks? There must have been at least three last week, and that was just during our lunch break." Reggie stared into the distance and said, "What if this parcel is a part of his evil plan? He could be building a nuclear weapon in the basement."

Hilda tried to be the voice of reason, but she had to agree with Reggie. Mr Nitwhitt was vile. He was the kind of person who would make babies cry just by entering the room. He had no friends. No girlfriend. No mobile phone. He lived in the school basement. Although it wasn't out-of-bounds no one dared to go down there. Not even the teachers. Hilda had heard hundreds of rumours about the caretaker, and although she didn't trust hearsay and gossip, some of them had to be true.

Hilda took a deep breath and said, "You're right." She picked up the parcel and added, "Someone needs to check he isn't up to no good. And I think it's a job for the super nerds."

Reggie nodded. "A reconnaissance mission. Let's deliver the parcel and look for suspicious activity. Maybe we'll find out what all the parcels are for?"

As the pair packed up their belongings and headed for the school basement, the wind built in strength and raindrops bounced off the playground tarmac. A storm cloud was forming over the school that was not going anywhere.

The only thing that was missing was the sinister cackle of a madman and a well-timed flash of lightning. But we'll get to that soon enough.

CHAPTER FOUR
JUNGLE

"But I thought this was the entrance to the basement?"

The pair stood in front of a hatch sticking out of the ground. The handles had chains wrapped around them and were locked by several padlocks. Metal bolts the size of those big tubes of sweets you only get at Christmas were bolted shut. Warning signs covered both hatch doors. It looked as

welcoming as a skunk's
rear-end.

"This is where Mr
Nitwhitt goes after school.
What do we do now?"

Reggie removed a pouch from his tool belt
and pulled out some tiny little instruments.
"I've been looking forward to trying out
these lock picking tools for ages. You keep a
lookout and I'll start fiddling."

"Can't we just try again tomorrow? Or
leave the parcel at the school reception?"

"No," replied Reggie as he inserted the
tiny piece of metal and tinkered with the
lock as they do on the TV Shows he was not
supposed to watch. "Remember the mission.
We need to make sure the caretaker isn't
a supervillain building a weapon of mass

destruction that he plans to test on school children."

"I know, I know. The greater good and all that superhero mumbo jumbo." Hilda looked around while nervously fiddling with her coat zip. "Just hurry up. I was hoping to finish memorising the letter 'F' in my encyclopaedias today."

The metal instrument snapped in Reggie's hand. "Drat! Remind me to add bolt cutters to my Christmas list."

"Look," said Hilda as she pointed to the warning sign in the top righthand corner.

Reggie read the sign out loud.

IF YOU HEAR SCREAMING
FROM BEHIND THIS DOOR,
DO NOT BE ALARMED. JUST BE
THANKFUL IT IS NOT YOU!

"No, the one next to that sign."

> STOP ASKING ME IF I'D LIKE
> TO TAKE PART IN THE TEACHER'S
> SECRET SANTA, BARBARA.
> I HATE CHRISTMAS AND I HATE
> SECRETS AND I ALSO HATE ALL
> TEACHERS, ESPECIALLY ONES CALLED
> BARBARA!

"No, no. On the other side."

An arrow pointed to the left. They both looked towards a darkened walkway of tree branches and jungle vines. Yes, it was extremely odd that a jungle was on the school premises.

> PLEASE LEAVE
> PARCELS BY THE
> OTHER ENTRANCE
> AT THE CENTRE
> OF THE
> **JUNGLE MAZE
> OF ETERNAL
> TORMENT**
> ←

Neither of them knew about it. You'd think it would be the kind of thing the council would discourage, but there it was, a tropical jungle right next to the school.

"Reggie, you still got that flashlight in your tool belt?"

Reggie clicked the torch on. "Way ahead of you, Hilda."

"Great, I'll stay here and finish 'F' while you find that other entrance."

"Come on," replied Reggie as he grabbed Hilda's arm and dragged her towards the

jungle.

He knew his friend well.

She always needed a friendly nudge to start an adventure, but once she was on her way, there was no stopping her.

As they entered the jungle maze, it instantly turned into summer. We're not talking English summer that couldn't even sizzle an egg. It was tropical heat that could sizzle the fake eyebrows off your grandma.

It
even sounded like
a jungle, with
insect chattering and running
water and mysterious rustling noises in
the distance. They followed the path as it
snaked from left to right until they reached
a fork in the path.

"Which way should we go?"

Hilda scratched her head. "Not sure. Let's
try that way."

As they stepped to the right, an
enormous snake dangled down from
the jungle canopy and hissed at them.

Hilda didn't need to check her
encyclopedias

to know it was venomous. You could tell
from the colours and stripes and creepy look
in its eye.

"On second thoughts, let's go the other
way."

They took a step back and turned to the
left. As they did so, the deadly growl of
a tiger greeted them. Hilda didn't need
to check her encyclopedia to know it was
a tiger, she'd been to the zoo and eaten
Frosties before. You could tell it was
hungry from the drool pouring out of
its mouth

full of sharpy, pointy teeth.

The best friends gripped each other's hand tightly. Being a super nerd was great for completing the Sunday crossword in under ten minutes and knowing all the answers at the end-of-year school test. When it comes to battling wild jungle animals, superior intellect was as useful as a cocktail umbrella in a tornado. The only silver lining was that 'death by poisonous snake bites and tiger wounds' would make for the most interesting gravestone in the cemetery.

The tiger took a step forward.

The snake curled back, ready to strike.

Hilda and Reggie closed their eyes.

THEN SOMETHING HAPPENED . . .

. . . but it was so unexpected and totally silly that I'll need a whole new chapter to explain it.

CHAPTER FiVE
ATTACK

Where were we?

Oh yes! It's time for something unexpected to happen.

Suddenly, something leapt out of the brushes. It was an extremely hairy man. Rags hung from his body and his beard stretched all the way to the floor. He stood in front of the kids and stared into the eyes of the deadly predators.

Hilda and
Reggie couldn't believe what
was happening as they watched
the jungle man attack the snake
and the tiger. And now that something
unexpected has happened, it's time for the
silly thing.

The jungle man didn't throw a spear.

DEADLY
PHOTO!

He didn't thrust a sword.

He didn't fire a gun.

Instead, he held up a *photo*.

The snake hissed and slithered back up
the branch. The tiger whimpered and backed
away slowly. The man followed the beast,
shouting and heckling it as it turned and
ran away. The man then returned his deadly
weapon to his satchel and turned to the kids.

"That was a close one," said their mystery

saviour.

"Thank you . . . er, Jungle Man," replied Hilda, her mouth completely dry from the unexpected and silly experience. "But how did you scare them off?"

"Tigers are fierce, and snakes are deadly, but all the animal kingdom fear the evil shelled beast that lurks in the darkness."

"Can we see it?" said Reggie with the curiosity of a thousand nosey neighbours.

"You are truly brave, children. But I must warn you, after staring into the eyes of the beast, you will never be the same person again. For the shelled monster is evil. There is no other creature on God's green earth that is as vile and monstrous. Are you sure?"

They both nodded.

"So be it." The man then removed the photo and unravelled it in front of their eyes.

It was a photo of a **SNAIL.**

THE EVIL SHELLED BEAST THAT LURKS IN THE DARKNESS

"Is that it?" said Hilda.

"Yeah, I was expecting more teeth," said Reggie.

"Don't be a fool. They may seem harmless and slow and easily squished, but you saw that tiger fleeing with its tail between its legs. Promise me if you ever meet one, you will run. Run and don't look back."

"Er, ok. We promise." Hilda gave a quick glance to her friend to check he was on the same page. Yep, they both thought this guy was as loopy as a ten-mile-long rollercoaster.

The mystery man rolled up the snail photo and said, "So, how long have you been here for then?"

Hilda checked her watch and said, "around five minutes."

"Lucky you. I've been stuck here for five years."

WHAT?
FiVE YEARS?!!

replied Reggie, in shock.

"I only came in here to deliver a parcel." He pointed at the tatty Royal Mail badge on his shirt and then showed the kids his red delivery bag. "The basement hatch was locked, so I followed the instructions and went into the jungle to find the other entrance. Five years later, I'm still trying to find it."

"We'll take it."

Hilda snapped her head towards Reggie.

"What?"

"I said we'll happily take the parcel off your hands. We're also delivering a parcel, so it's no trouble. Just point us in the direction you think the other entrance is and we'll point you to the exit."

The delivery man fell to his knees as tears dribbled down his face. "Thank you, oh, thank you, kind children. I haven't seen my family in five years. I gave up all hope long ago and thought I'd waste away in this jungle. I shall name my children after you. I will erect a statue in my front garden to proclaim this good deed. I shall get a tattoo on my . . ."

"Sorry to interrupt," said Hilda. "But we're on our lunch break. Afternoon class starts in

twenty-five minutes, so we really must get going."

The man stood to his feet and immediately hugged both of them. "Yes, of course. Take these." He gave Reggie the delivery bag containing the parcel and Hilda the photo of the snail. "A token of my appreciation."

"Er, thanks, I suppose?" said Hilda. It was probably the strangest gift she had ever received. It even beat the socks with carrots wearing bow ties she got for Christmas from Aunt Maggie last year.

"Keep going left and you'll hear terrifying sounds," said the delivery man. "I was never brave enough to investigate that area."

"Thanks," replied Reggie. "Just keep going that way and you'll reach the exit in five minutes."

Propelled with sheer joy, the postman leapt into the air and sped off.

CHAPTER SIX
SNOW

"What do you think is in this other parcel?"

Reggie hacked at a jungle vine as they trekked onwards towards the howling sound. He stopped to drink some water, then replied, "Not sure. Shall we look?"

He pulled out the parcel, and they both leaned in for a closer look.

"It looks pretty similar to me." Hilda put

her ear next to it. It made her ear glow. "It even sounds the same."

Reggie pulled out the first parcel, held them next to each other. "You're right. Same size. Same packaging. Same glow and sound. They're identical."

Then they both vibrated. The eerie glow grew and faded away in sync. Reggie moved them away from each other and they stopped. Then held them together, and the pulsing started again. "How curious," said Reggie. "They seem to enjoy being next to each other."

"Maybe we should keep them separate," said Hilda as she took one parcel and put it in her backpack. "We don't know what is inside them yet. It looks pretty, but it could mean trouble."

"I agree," replied Reggie, as he returned his parcel to the delivery bag and went back to hacking jungle vines. "I'm starting to think they are energy sources, like batteries. The more you have, the stronger the energy output. But I wonder what the caretaker needs the energy source for?"

"Maybe he is an inventor?" said Hilda. "He could be on the verge of a scientific breakthrough that could change the

world?"

"Or destroy it?" replied Reggie. "Don't forget who we are talking about here. The man who was allegedly expelled from school when he was a pupil for blowing up the science lab. The man who played a yeti in a low-budget horror movie. The man who collects *snails*."

"They're just rumours," said Hilda. She liked to look for good in people, which admittedly was an impossible task with the caretaker. "We should reserve judgement until we

see inside his basement."

"I used to think he just loved eating snails on toast. But now I'm starting to think that Mr Nitwhitt is *actually* creating a snail army in his basement. The Snail Army of Doom! I know it sounds ridiculous. But so does going on a jungle trek in our lunch break." As Reggie hacked another vine, it fell to the floor. But this one was covered in snow.

They both looked at the snow on the ground. Then looked up at what was in front of them. Then looked at each other in confusion.

"Are you seeing what I'm seeing?"

"Yep," replied Hilda. "We're no longer in a jungle."

They took a step forward. The snow crunched under their shoes. A bitter wind slapped them in the face. Massive snowflakes fell from the sky and dribbled down their necks. They were entering a snowstorm of epic proportions. It was a welcome break from the heat of the jungle, but after five seconds their skeletons shivered, and their brains turned on the de-mist setting. They needed to find shelter from the storm before they became snowmen.

"Look, over there," shouted Reggie over the winds.

"Is that a hatch?" replied Hilda as frost formed on her tonsils.

The kids ran towards the hatch.

Pulling the freezing cold handle,
they stumbled into darkness. Reggie
closed the hatch with a loud bang that
echoed down a long hallway. The
lighting was low. The air quality
was mediocre. The creepiness rating
was sky high. But anything was
better than being in a snowstorm
without thermal underwear.

Then a high-pitched scream
echoed through the hallway.
It was a haunting sound that
sent a shiver down their
spines, which travelled all
the way to their little
toes. Hilda reached for
the hatch, but Reggie
stopped her. "We can't

turn
around
now. Not after
coming this far."

Hilda wanted to ignore Reggie,
but she knew he was right. Class can
wait. This was more important. She turned
around and started walking down the
hallway. Reggie clicked his flashlight to
light the way. Several rats scurried away
as they continued their parcel delivery
mission.

The super nerds whispered to each other.
Reggie would ask the questions and Hilda

Q: IN HARRY POTTER, WHERE DOES VERNON DURSLEY WORK?

would give him the answers, often word for word from her encyclopaedia. Whenever Reggie found a question she couldn't answer, she resisted the urge to unzip her backpack. It was a welcome distraction from what they were currently doing — trespassing in the caretaker's mysterious basement.

After ten minutes of walking, they finally reached a closed door. Reggie read the sign in big red lettering.

"This is getting ridiculous," said Hilda.

IF YOU ARE THE SCHOOL CARETAKER, WELCOME TO
THE SNAIL EXPERIMENTAL TESTING LABORATORY.

IF YOU ARE A SNAIL, IGNORE WHAT YOU HAVE JUST
READ AND WELCOME TO
THE SNAIL LUXURY SPA AND HOTEL.

IF YOU ARE NEITHER, THERE IS NOTHING TO SEE
HERE, SO TURN AROUND AND **GO HOME.**

"I know," replied Reggie. "I'm pretty sure snails can't read. He really doesn't need to put up all these lengthy signs. Come on. I'll open this one." Reggie nudged the door carefully. It slowly edged open, revealing concrete stairs descending into shadow.

A: VERNON DURSLEY IS A DIRECTOR OF A FIRM CALLED GRUNNINGS, WHICH MAKES DRILLS.

CHAPTER SEVEN
LAB

"How many stairs does this basement have?"

Reggie stopped to catch his breath. "Too many."

Hilda and Reggie slowly tiptoed down, further and further, deeper and deeper in the belly of the caretaker's layer. It was as dark and cold as a headteacher's soul. In the distance, a faint glow welcomed them. As they slowly approached,

the yellowy-green light became stronger
and a humming noise enter their ears and
vibrated all the way around their bodies.

They silently stepped off the last step and
cautiously entered the lab.

It was a large room, full of equipment
and tools and gadgets and gizmos and
contraptions and devices. In the centre stood
a massive machine. It dominated the room.
The glowing and the humming were coming
from it. Reggie's eyes were full of awe and
wonder. Without caution or care, he walked
up to it, never taking his eyes off it, and
stroked it.

"Reggie, what are you doing?"

"Beautiful, isn't it?" replied Reggie. "It's like someone has plucked it straight from my dreams."

"But he could be down here right now," she whispered, glancing around the room as she slowly approached.

"You take a look around. I'll get to work figuring out what the caretaker is building."

Hilda didn't bother trying to argue with him. She knew him well enough to know that this was what he lived for — tinkering with machinery. He was a world-class tinkerer. She had no doubt that, one day, he'd become an engineer, but she liked to think that with her intellectual influence she could guide him towards being a molecular or aerospace or nanorobotics engineer.

Once she was sure that they were alone, Hilda started snooping around. There were hundreds of discarded gizmos. All unfinished and abandoned. The caretaker must have been working on this project for years. A thought popped into her head.

I wonder if he is close to finishing...

WHATEVER HE IS DOING???

A desk caught her attention. She walked over to the workspace and saw an old-looking computer and piles and piles of notebooks. As she scanned through the notebooks for clues, she noticed something moving out of the corner of her eye.

"Er . . . Reggie. You better come over here. Right now."

"But I'm busy," shouted Reggie, who had his head and shoulders inside the machine with a wrench in one hand and a torch in the other.

"This can't wait," replied Hilda.

Reggie huffed as he returned his tools to his tool belt and found Hilda. She was staring at a gigantic glass jar full of black stuff. It was twice as high as the kids and as wide as a blue whale's bottom. "What? What

was so important that you needed to disturb my important tinkering?"

Hilda's bottom lip wobbled as she slowly lifted her hand to point at the jar.

Reggie stepped closer to the jar. "What's in there?"

"I think I know, but I don't want to be right about this one."

"No, it can't be. But . . . that's awful."

Thousands and thousands of snails were wiggling around the jar. They were trapped inside the jar and were swimming in their own slime. It was a disgusting sight of animal cruelty. "So, at least we know one rumour is true."

"Yeah, Mr Nitwhitt definitely collects snails."

Reggie added, "And he is creating a..."

"That we don't know," replied Hilda. "But I think I might have found something in one of his notebooks that could help us work out what the machine is for."

Reggie looked at the wall behind the caretaker's desk and replied, "no need for a little notebook. I've just found his 'Evil Plan of Epic Proportions to Destroy the School and Annihilate the Pupils and Obliterate Barbara Forever and Ever'."

"This isn't the time for one of your jokes, Reggie."

"No, really. Look."

Hilda looked and let out a gasp. There it was. A huge blueprint of the machine in all its sinister glory. The massive wallboard had a title, and to Reggie's credit, it was word for word what he said. Except for the bit he missed that was in brackets '(working title for my wonderful creation—*The School Subjugator*)'.

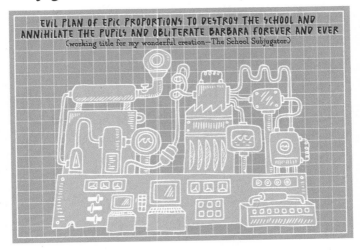

Hilda's left eye twitched. That happened when she read a word she didn't understand.

"Come on," said Reggie as he put his tools back into his tool belt. "I think we've been here long enough. Let's get going."

Hilda ignored him and took off her backpack. She rummaged around and then pulled out volume seven of her encyclopaedias. "This can't wait."

"Seriously?" replied Reggie. "You know I love all your silly quirks, but this isn't the time to learn a new word. We need to leave. Now!"

Hilda ignored him. "I'll find out what it means while you work out how to free the snails."

Reggie rubbed his temples. "Why do I get the feeling this is a bad idea?"

"We can't just leave them here like that. Use your hammer."

"But then the caretaker will know that someone has been in his basement. I don't think we want to make him our enemy, Hilda. Plus, don't forget the photo! *The evil shelled beast that lurks in the darkness.* There are probably thousands of them in there."

Hilda looked up from her encyclopaedia and wiggled her eyebrows to plead her case in defence of the poor little snails. Reggie huffed. "I hate how you are always right."

He pulled out his hammer and took aim at what he thought was the weakest area of the giant jar. He drew his arm back to strike the

glass as hard as he could. But just as he was about to deliver the liberating blow, his arm wouldn't move.

He hadn't frozen solid.

He hadn't become a pacifist.

He didn't need any persuading to set the snails free from their glass cage.

Reggie's arm wouldn't budge because an old, wrinkled hand was holding it back.

CHAPTER EIGHT
CARETAKER

"It seems I have some uninvited guests," said Mr Nitwhitt as he paced around his basement.

With a name like Nitwhitt, you'd expect him to be the punchline of a joke, but oh no, this fellow is the complete opposite. He is a joke without a punchline.

The caretaker was extremely tall and thin. He looked like a rake with strange haircut. His pointy nose looks like a twisted coathanger. His beedy eyes look like tiny mouse droppings. And good luck trying to make him giggle. He's as ticklish as a gravestone. But his oddest quirk? I'll let him explain that one.

"I never imagined that two kids would discover my plans and attempt to stop me. I thought all the pupils at Churchill Junior School were as stupid and insignificant as a single, discarded raisin."

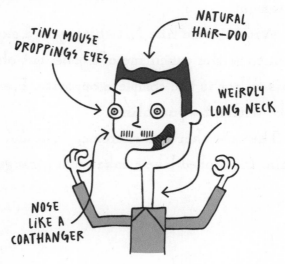

NATURAL HAIR-DOO

TINY MOUSE DROPPINGS EYES

WEIRDLY LONG NECK

NOSE LIKE A COATHANGER

Reggie and Hilda had a very brief conversation using only their eyebrows. They decided not to say anything that might make their situation any worse than it already was. Mr Nitwhitt had strapped them to a table, tilted towards him, and was grinning with delight. Why stray from the classic bad guy stuff? No need to reinvent the wheel for restraining the good guys and blabbing about your evil plans.

"You came very close. Any more of your childish tinkering could have set me back by a month. It would have been a heap of junk not even capable of making my morning cappuccino. But it turns out you have been most helpful. I was two power crystals short, and you kindly hand delivered them in person."

Reggie really wanted to say something. Hilda frantically wiggled her eyebrows, but it was no use. He was staring at the mad scientist with rage in his eyes.

"In other circumstances, I would offer you a job as my assistants. You both have brilliant minds capable of doing brilliant things. But, sadly, I work alone. However, you have the privilege of front row seats to witness my machine unleash its godlike superpower on your worthless school."

Reggie's face was turning red. He was biting his tongue to stop it from talking. Hilda knew trying to stop him now was futile.

"You see, dear little meddlesome children, I have been experimenting with nature. Picking up where God stopped for a break. The natural world is unimaginably beautiful and wildly destructive. Soon, I will control nature itself. Nothing will stop me."

Reggie couldn't hold it in any longer.

YOU TALK TOO MUCH!

"I'm sorry. What did you say?"

"I said you love the sound of your own voice. You should quit this mad scientist stuff and become a podcaster instead. And who wants a Snail Army of Doom, anyway?

It's pathetic."

"Pardon?" replied Mr Nitwhitt in bewilderment.

"You heard me. Collecting all those poor little snails so that you can zap them with your machine and create a horde of mutant, killer snails eager to do your bidding."

"Oh my," said the caretaker as he let out a disappointed sigh. "Is that what you think I am doing?"

"Don't play dumb with us," replied Reggie.

Mr Nitwhitt shook his head. "Well, in that case, I take back everything I said. You aren't intelligent, after all. You're just as stupid as the rest of the mindless ants scuttling around that stupid school."

"I'm sorry. What did you say?" replied

PLEASE DON'T TURN ME
INTO A MUTANT KILLER SNAIL

Reggie.

"Snail Army of Doom? I've never heard anything so ridiculously silly in my life."

"But the snails," said Hilda. "Why have you been collecting snails and keeping them hidden away in a giant glass jar?"

"What? This thing?" replied the caretaker as he walked over to the snails. "That's my snack jar."

Reggie and Hilda's jaws dropped.

"Building a machine that will destroy the school and everyone in it is hungry work." Mr Nitwhitt climbed up a ladder, opened the jar, plucked out a snail and sucked it out of its shell.

Reggie and Hilda quickly closed their

THE
SUPER VILLAINS
SNACK JAR

CHEW SQUISH GULP!

mouths, then threw up a little. And again, as they heard a squishy noise as the caretaker chewed.

"Did you know a snail has all the nutrients needed for a balanced diet?"

"Please, stop," said Hilda.

"You just need to remove the crunchy bit and then they are perfectly edible. And quite tasty."

"No more, please," said Reggie.

"I sense you are enjoying this conversation, so I'll also let you know that sometimes, as a special treat, I'll spread a few snails on a slice of toast and wash it down with a glass of strawberry milk."

Reggie and Hilda's stomachs grumbled.

Not an 'oh-that-sounds-tasty,' kind of grumble. It was an 'eat-snails-on-toast-and-I'll-make-you-poop-so-fast-and-violently-you'll-never-be-able-to-poop-again,' kind of grumble.

"For the record," said Hilda. "I was never on board with the Snail Army of Doom theory. That was all Reggie."

"Hilda," said Reggie to his friend. "Let's not squabbled. We need to work together if we're going to get out of this."

"But you won't. You failed. I have placed the power crystals into my machine. It has been repaired and is now at 100% power. And now you are strapped to a table with a giant laser pointing at you."

"What giant laser?" replied Reggie.

"This one," said Nr Nitwhitt as he

pressed a small red button. The machine suddenly transformed in front of their eyes into a giant laser. It was the scariest thing they had ever seen (and don't forget the tiger and venomous snake from the jungle. That was pretty scary!)

"I shouldn't have asked." Reggie reached

the point of no return and added, "And I suppose I shouldn't also ask you this follow-up question. If that red button wasn't the one that turns the machine on, then which one is?"

"This one," said Mr Nitwhitt as he wheeled over a massive red button on wheels the size of an overweight watermelon.

"Ok, now that's more like it," said Hilda. "We're doomed."

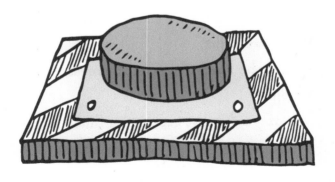

CHAPTER NINE

HURRICANE

The storm outside continued to rage on. The wind was so loud that it could be heard through the walls of the basement. The lightning was so close, when it struck the ground, the entire room flashed with electric blue light.

Inside the basement, the conversation also raged on.

"So, if you're not creating a Snail Army

of Doom," said Reggie. "What are you doing?"

Mr Nitwhitt was about to continue his evil genius monologue. An endless string of self-inflating nonsense to puff his ego into the heavens, but Hilda thankfully interrupted him. "The machine can control the weather."

"Very good, little girl. You do have a brain in that tiny skull of yours."

Hilda knew that was not meant as a compliment, but she was very happy Mr Nitwhitt had changed his opinion of her. Hilda continued talking to cement her intelligence in the conversation. "The jungle was a failed experiment. So was the snowstorm. You don't want to create a new environment. You

want to create *extreme weather.*"

"Very, very good," replied the caretaker. "You are correct. This is a weather machine. I created the jungle by mistake, but the snowstorm was no accident. It was a steppingstone towards what I will create today."

Mr Nitwhitt began pacing in front of the restrained children in that trademarked mad scientist's walk: a slow, sinister walk that echoed around the room while drumming his fingers together in pleasure. "When I tested the laser on a harmless cloud, it created a permanent tropical sub climate next to the school. Not exactly what I was hoping for. The jungle soon sprouted up, and I added

a few tigers and snakes to liven up the place. When I tested the laser on a snow cloud, it created a permanent snowstorm. I had to invest in under floor heating and thermal underpants, but my machine was finally working. It was on the way to creating the perfect storm."

Reggie rolled his eyes. "Seriously, you really do talk too much!"

"I know," smiled the caretaker. "It's one of the perks of the job. That and all the snails I can eat."

Hilda glowed with pride. She had worked it out. But she was also terrified at what might happen next. "So now that you have created the perfect storm," she said, not wanting to finish her question, "what happens next?"

"Oy, little girl. That's where you are mistaken." He walked closer to the children and said, "This is just your average storm. But when I use my weather machine and fire my giant laser at this storm cloud, it will become a . . .

Reggie and Hilda's eyebrows did a synchronised routine. Up, up again and slight wobble at the very top. When translated to English, it meant "uh-oh!"

"Just imagine," said the caretaker with a smile plastered across his smug face. "I'll

have my very own hurricane. I can hire
it out to the highest bidder, like a bouncy
castle at birthday parties. Dictators from
all around the world will call me up asking
for my services. Of course, the first thing
I'll do is test out its destructive capabilities
by setting it on a collision course with
Churchill Junior School."

Reggie gulped, then said, "But won't
the hurricane also destroy your basement
laboratory?"

"No," replied the caretaker. "We're too
far underground. Hurricanes specialise in
destroying everything and anything above

ground, but one thing they can't do is go downstairs." Mr Nitwhitt rubbed his hands together, then added, "I think it's time to *test the machine.*"

Hilda gulped. "But if you test it on us, you won't have enough power left to create the hurricane."

"Wrong again," replied the caretaker as he made sure the laser was pointing directly at the children. "You helpfully delivered two power crystals to me yesterday. Even you can do that math: one crystal to zap you two and one crystal to zap the storm cloud."

Reggie turned to Hilda. "At least it probably won't hurt."

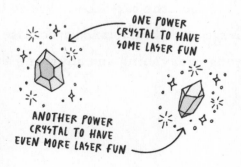

ONE POWER CRYSTAL TO HAVE SOME LASER FUN

ANOTHER POWER CRYSTAL TO HAVE EVEN MORE LASER FUN

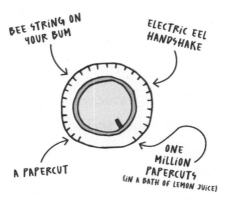

BEE STRING ON YOUR BUM

ELECTRIC EEL HANDSHAKE

A PAPERCUT

ONE MILLION PAPERCUTS (IN A BATH OF LEMON JUICE)

"Good point," said the caretaker as he walked up to his computer. "I'll turn up the pain intensity levels to full power."

Hilda turned to Reggie. "Maybe the headteacher will work it out and save us."

"Not likely," replied the caretaker as he clicked a button on his keyboard to reveal a security camera in the headteacher's office. "She always has a cream cake at this time in the day. See for yourself."

Reggie and Hilda watched as the one person who could save them was happily enjoying a custard slice and a cup of tea. "Well, maybe someone will call," said Reggie.

"There's a chance a student will throw up in Barbara's shoes again."

"Ah yes, I'll take care of that," replied Mr Nitwhitt as he picked up his caretaker's phone and recorded a new answer machine message. "I'm sorry I can't come to the phone right now. I'm currently in the middle of creating the most terrifying hurricane this world has ever seen. Please leave your message after I have destroyed the school and I'll never get back to you."

Hilda looked the caretaker in the eyes and said, "Please, don't do this. Surely you have a conscience. Didn't your parents teach you to be kind to each other and, you know, not zap defenceless children and cause mass destruction?"

"Oh drat," replied the caretaker. "You're right." He reached for a photo frame on his desk of his parents' and began talking to it. "What you don't know won't hurt you. Anyway, I promise to buy you that sit on lawnmower you've always wanted when I'm filthy rich." He put the photo frame back, this time facing away from the scene of the crime.

It was Reggie's turn to give it a go. "Please, if you zap defenceless children, the guilt will haunt you for the rest of your life."

"Way ahead of you," replied the caretaker. "I'll donate 10p a month to a children's charity. That should even things out nicely."

SERIOUSLY?! IS THAT IT???

Reggie and Hilda had run out of ideas. Their shoulders slouched down as all hope drained away. Reggie said some words of comfort to his friend, "well, at least we tried. We can die with dignity knowing we did our best."

"Oh yes, I almost forgot," replied the caretakers as he rummaged around his laboratory for something. Then he returned, put two silly hats on the kids' heads, and took a selfie with a polaroid camera. "How could I have forgotten to take a picture? I'll cherish this moment forever. I'm going to put it in my supervillain scrapbook."

Mr Nitwhitt skipped to his desk and began cutting and sticking and throwing glitter everywhere.

Reggie looked at Hilda. She was wearing a sombrero with a stick-on moustache. Hilda looked at Reggie. He was wearing a wizard's hat with a grey beard hooked around his ears.

This was it. The end of the line. All hope was gone. This must have been the lowest, most disheartened moment of their lives. But then they noticed something.

A tiny slither of hope.

An unlikely hero.

A small chance to be rescued.

On the ground, crawling across the floor, was one solitary snail.

CHAPTER TEN
LAST REQUEST

One snail had escaped and was heading for
Mr Nitwhitt's computer.

The caretaker must have forgotten to shut
it and now one snail had made a break for
it. If the escapee could get to the computer
console and wriggle over the keyboard,
maybe it could cause the machine to short
circuit. There was just one problem. The
snail was only halfway there. Even at full

speed, a snail is the slowest living thing in the animal kingdom.

They had to stall for time.

"Before you press the big, red button," said Hilda. "You must tell me who your interior designer is. I love what you've done with this space. What colour paint did you put on the walls?"

"I didn't," said the caretaker, still working on his scrapbook. "It's a mixture of snail slime splatter and sweat."

"Oh, how lovely," replied Hilda. "Well, I like it. Brings out the evil in your eyes."

"Done," said Mr Nitwhitt as he closed his scrapbook and reached for the button.

"Wait," said Reggie. "I think you should

take the photo again. I'm pretty sure I blinked."

The caretaker tried to resist, but the urge for perfection was too strong. No one wants a blinking child in their 'Journey to Becoming the World's Most Diabolical Supervillain Scrapbook'. He picked up the book and looked at the photo. "No, you both look perfectly silly. And not a blink in sight."

Just before Mr Nitwhitt reached the button, Reggie added, "Haven't you forgotten something?"

"No," replied Mr Nitwhitt. "The crystals are loaded, the machine is at full power, the

JOURNEY TO BECOMING
THE WORLD'S MOST
DIABOLICAL SUPERVILLAIN SCRAPBOOK

scrapbook entry is complete, and I've had my afternoon snack."

"Yes, but you haven't let us have our last request."

"Exactly," added Hilda. "You wouldn't be a very good supervillain if you didn't let your victims have a last request."

"Fine," replied the caretaker as he slumped into his chair. "What do you want?"

"I'd like to hear my entire collection of encyclopaedias one last time," said Hilda. "Would you read all twelve volumes aloud to me?"

DENIED

"I'm famished. Could I have one last meal," said Reggie. "A full Christmas dinner, please. With all the trimmings."

DECLINED

"How about one last dance?" said Hilda. "Of course, we don't know how to dance, so you'd have to teach us first. Either salsa dancing or the foxtrot, you can choose."

REJECTED

"I've never been on a holiday," said Reggie. "I hear Hawaii is lovely this time of year."

REFUSED

"Hilda would also love to know what the word 'subjugator' means."

NOBODY KNOWS

The caretaker got to his feet and started walking towards the button. "It's just a fancy made-up word to make you sound more intelligent. And if this next request isn't a serious one, you will have used up all my patience."

"Well," said Hilda with sincerity in her voice. "If you really want to know what we'd like, then I think you'll be very surprised and happy to grant it."

"Go on, I'm listening."

"All we want is the opportunity to go to university," said Reggie as honesty as he could. "I want to go to the Massachusetts Institute of Technology in America to study Engineering and Hilda wants to go to Oxford University in England to study

English."

Mr Nitwhitt rubbed his forehead. He was developing one of those crippling migraines only children can inflict upon adults. He stomped towards the button in rage with his hand stretched outwards.

shouted the kids.

The caretaker stopped. His foot hovered over the snail, that was over halfway to reaching the computer console. Reggie quickly said, "we'll settle for a glass of water."

"That's more like it," said the caretaker. He moved his boot towards the doorway and started walking towards his kitchen. "Wait right here."

"Don't forget the ice," added Hilda.

"And a slice of lemon and one of those tiny umbrellas for me, please," added Reggie.

Mr Nitwhitt walked out of his laboratory muttering curse words adults specifically reserve for annoying children. Reggie and Hilda then looked at their rescuer. But something was wrong. It was slithering past the computer.

"What are you doing?" whispered Hilda, as loudly as she could. "Turn back. Go for the computer desk."

"Please, hurry," added Reggie. "We can't keep this up for much longer. If you crawl over the keyboard, there is a chance you'll break it so he can't create the super hurricane."

But the snail wasn't listening.

It carried on its path.

That's when they both realised they had been stalling the caretaker for some else's escape plan, not their own.

The snail was heading towards the exit.

CHAPTER ELEVEN
BIG RED BUTTON

When Mr Nitwhitt returned to his laboratory, the snail had reached the first step and was slowly travelling up the second. He stomped up to the kids, strapped to the table with a giant laser pointing at them, and slammed their glasses of water on the ground. He then turned around and headed to the big red button.

"But our arms are tied down," said

Reggie. "How do you expect us to drink like this?"

"I don't," replied the caretaker. He had found his smile again as he grinned madly at the kids. "You asked for a glass of water. You said nothing about helping you drink it. And now that I've completed your last requests, I can finally *test my machine.*"

Reggie couldn't watch. He closed his eyes.

Hilda couldn't either. She looked to the side.

Mr Nitwhitt intended to watch every second. He moved his hand and hovered it over the button.

TEENY TINY GAP (0.02mm)

"I've been looking forward to doing this for a very long time," said the caretaker. "To create your very own super hurricane is a very special moment. But first, let's see what happens when you zap two kids with my weather machine."

A tiny click echoed around the basement.

CLICK

To everyone's surprise, it was not the click of a button.

It was more of a squidgy kind of click.

They all looked towards the sound. The escapee snail was reversing back in its shell. The tiny manoeuvre was complete with a

satisfying pop.

The next sound they all heard was the caretaker's belly rumble.

Mr Nitwhitt walked over to the snail, plucked it off the ground and throw it back into his snack jar. "I'll eat you later. Right now, I've got more important things to do than have a snack." Mr Nitwhitt grabbed his duct tape and climbed the ladder, closing the lid and tapping it shut.

"Well, where was I?" said the caretaker. "Oh, yes". He then walked over to Reggie and Hilda and duct taped their mouths shut. "I don't know why I didn't do that earlier. Never mind."

The storm raged on and on outside as the lunch bell rang out across the playground. All the teachers were wonkily parking their

cars in the carpark. All the
pupils were walking back into
school, counting down the
seconds to the end of the
day. The headteacher was wiping
the custard from her mouth and making her
sixth cup of tea.

But, as you already know, there are
two pupils and a caretaker who are doing
something else. Something completely and
utterly mad. Something that could only
happen in a comic book or an apocalyptic TV
series or a silly cartoon with a catchy theme
tune.

But remember this, dear reader:

- Comic books have superheroes
- Apocalyptic TV series have
  producers who are strongly against

televising child torture.

- And silly cartoons with catchy
  theme tunes tend to steer clear of
  mass murder and mindless violence.
  Plus, they try not to kill off the
  main characters.

Meanwhile, the evil villain of this story,
Mr Nitwhitt, gleefully walked over to the
big, red button and said, "It's time to be
zapped."

CHAPTER TWELVE

SNAILS
(AGAIN)

Here are three common facts about snails:

1. Snails have been on this planet for longer than the dinosaurs.

2. They have no teeth. Instead, they have thousands of microscopic tooth-like lumps on their bellies that grind up their food.

3. They are completely harmless.

THE FIRST ONE IS CORRECT.
THE SECOND IS A COMMON MISCONCEPTION.
THE THIRD IS UTTER POPPYCOCK.

Archaeologists think that the Tyrannosaurus Rex was at the top of the food chain.

WRONG!

The prehistoric snail ruled the Jurassic Period. Carnivores never nibbled them, and herbivores always left them the best leaves. In fact, the snails decided the T-Rex needed to be taken down a notch and so employed them as their personal bodyguards.

Scientists think snails are simple organisms.

WRONG AGAIN!

KING OF
THE DINOSAURS

If a curious biologist were to dissect
a snail, they'd be in for a big shock.
Studying this highly evolved specimen
would completely revolutionize everything
we know about biology. One snail has more
razor-sharp teeth than a family of sharks
who regularly go to the dentist. They are
just very good at hiding them.

Historians think that the fall of the
Roman Empire was because of political power
struggles and a deadly pandemic.

WRONG AGAIN,
(AGAIN!)

The Romans conquered most of Europe
with their military strength and advanced
technologies. If the snails hadn't stepped in,

STUFF OF NIGHTMARES

they may have conquered the whole globe.

Snails are lethal killers, but they are also moral creatures who intervene when the scales of power needs rebalancing. So, they hide in plain sight. Only revealing their truly terrifying potential when absolutely necessary. They are the dormant platoon of evil law enforcers, ready to enact their unique form of justice on the world once a millennium.

And, if you read on, you'll witness such an event.

CLICK!

Mr Nitwhitt's evil laugh was loud enough to overpower the storm outside. He lifted his hand off the big red button and watched his creation spark to life. His eyes glowed green as the crystals powered up. The weather machine hummed as pure energy surged within the giant laser. The laser looked directly at its targets as a ball of green energy formed at the pointy end.

Reggie and Hilda watched in horror.

There was nothing they could do to stop it.

This was the end.

MUA-HA-HA-HA

The caretaker's evil laugh carried on, growing louder and louder. It filled the room and created the perfect atmosphere for zapping defenceless children into a pile of dust. The kids shut their eyes, much like most people do when having an injection. That way, you don't know when the moment of impact will be.

Reggie and Hilda waited for the end.

CRACK!

Reggie and Hilda opened one eye, but only a tiny bit.

The laser was still powering up. The caretaker was still absentmindedly laughing. The storm was still raging on outside. But none of those things made the cracking sound.

Only one thing in the room would make a cracking sound.

Then the giant glass jar cracked again. This time, it was much louder. A large crack journeyed across the circumference of the jar and finally reached back to its beginning.

Then the jar completely shattered.

CHAPTER THIRTEEN
JAILBREAK

Water instantly flooded the caretaker's basement laboratory.

Not with rainwater.

Or from a burst pipe.

Or with a lorry-load of fan mail from Japanese tourists.

The entire basement became flooded with a strange, slimy liquid. It glued Mr Nitwhitt to the spot. It made the weather machine

short-circuit and spark out of control. It
sent the computer console coco loco. Reggie
and Hilda and the caretaker all watched in
bewilderment as the snails worked as one.
They swam through the slime like majestic
penguins. They leapt from the slime like
magnificent dolphins. They encircled the
caretaker like intelligent killer whales.

"What's going on?" shouted Mr Nitwhitt
as he tried to move his legs. But it was no
use. All he could do was watch as the snails
merged into one mass. The massive black
thing emerged from the slime and towered
over the defenceless caretaker. It then
opened its mouth and roared. It sounded like
a choir of hungry dinosaurs with a chorus of
hungry lions in the background.

It was the animal all creatures feared

most. The thing we humans had long forgotten.

Reggie blinked. He did that whenever he thought he might be having a crazy dream. Or in this case, a terrifying nightmare.

Hilda violently shook her head. She did that whenever she saw something she couldn't explain with human logic or the knowledge in her encyclopaedias.

Then *the evil shelled beast that lurks in*

the darkness did three things:

1. It nudged the laser with its head.
2. It whacked the weather machine with its tail.
3. It swallowed the caretaker in one gulp.

Hilda looked at the laser. It was now pointing just to the left of them and looked like it was going to miss them. She then noticed steam rising from the machine. It had a massive dent where the giant snail hit it. Some very odd noises were coming from it. None of them were comforting. She then looked at the spot Mr Nitwhitt was standing in. It was now empty.

"Er, what do we do now?" said Hilda.

"Not a clue," replied Reggie. "But if I had the choice, I think I'd rather be zapped by a giant laser than eaten by a giant snail."

MULTIPLE CHOICE DEATH
PLEASE CHOOSE FROM THE FOLLOWING OPTIONS

 ☐　 ☐　 ☐

DEATH BY
GIANT LASER

DEATH BY
KILLER SNAIL

DEATH BY
SANDWICHES

"Well, unfortunately, this isn't a multiple-choice death." Hilda paused as the snail burped. Two black platform boots flew across the room. Then two snail eyes popped out of the black mass and turned to them. "Something tells me that thing has a big appetite."

"Hey, snail," yelled Reggie as he tried his best to wriggle out of his restraints. "I'm glad you enjoyed your starter. Maybe save us for pudding and eat the laser for your main course?"

The snail of doom tilted its head. The two large eyeballs, being held up by squidgy black stalks, didn't move. They stayed perfectly still, one looking at Reggie and the other at Hilda. It seemed to be considering Reggie's proposal. It then turned its body and slithered slowly towards them.

"You've enacted your revenge," yelled Hilda as she wriggled with all her might. "You've eaten the person who has been eating you. We've never eaten a snail, or even stepped on one. In fact, I saved a snail earlier today and gave it one of my crisps. Please, don't eat us."

The snail of doom stopped. Again, it tilted its head and looked as though it was mulling over the desperate plea to be spared. It then licked its lips and continued its slow march.

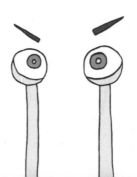

"I can't get myself free," shouted Reggie. "How about you?"

"It's no use," replied Hilda. "These restrains are too tight."

The snail of doom then stopped in front of the children. It opened its enormous mouth and roared. No living person has ever seen the insides of a snail's mouth and lived to tell the tale. Its jaws were the size of an open car boot. It was full of teeth, each as large and pointy as a giant's toothpick.

As the snail prepared to swallow them and the tables they were strapped to in one mouthful, Hilda stated the obvious.

THIS is OFFICIALLY THE WORST SCHOOL DAY IN THE HISTORY OF THE WORLD!

So, when the laser suddenly zapped a brilliant green beam, it wasn't much of a plot twist. Why not add another peril into the mix? The more the merrier.

The laser violently rumbled and then exploded. The brilliant green beam missed the kids and bounced around the basement. All of them, including the snail, couldn't take their eyes off the beautifully horrifying sight. It narrowly missed Reggie, then bounded off the machine. It stuck the table, inches from Hilda's leg, then bounced off the ceiling and floor several times. It hit the spot where Mr Nitwhitt had been standing, then ricocheted around the basement.

If anything, the beam was gaining momentum rather than slowing down. It was searching for something to strike. And it finally found its target when it smashed through the basement's only window and struck the storm cloud.

Suddenly, everything went green.

The rain turned green.

The storm cloud turned green.

And the lightning, yep, it was green too.

Three bolts of brilliant green erupted from the storm cloud. Lightning is normally random, forking across the sky in no particular direction without a purpose. But not this time.

The three bolts
glided through
the air. They weaved through
the sky, missing the trees and the
school building and even the basement
window frame. Why three? Well, the
answer is strikingly obvious.

3 LIGHTNING BOLTS FOR

3 TARGETS

CHAPTER FOURTEEN
LIGHTNING

The first bolt struck Reggie in the right arm. His entire body shook as the green energy buzzed in every molecule.

The second bolt struck Hilda in the head. Her hair fuzzed into a giant afro as the green energy wrapped itself around her.

The third bolt struck the snail of doom. It immediately exploded. Thousands of normal-sized snails flew across the basement in all directions, leaving a slime covered lump laying on the ground. Mr Nitwhitt glowed green as the bolt's energy surged through his body from head to toe and back to the head again.

The basement fell to a silence. There was a slight hum in the air as the three lightning casualties slowly turned from florescent green to their normal colour. Hilda turned her head towards her friend and said, "Reggie, you okay?"

"Yeah," he replied. "In fact, considering I was just struck by green lightning, I feel fantastic."

"I know," said Hilda as she flexed her finger. "Me too. But how could that be? Lightning contains one billion joules of energy. That's enough to power fifty-four houses for twenty-four hours."

"Er, Hilda, have you noticed something odd?"

"Did you also know," continued Hilda as she ignored her friend, "that they reach fifty-four thousand degrees, or in other words, roughly five times hotter than the surface of the sun?"

"Yeah, yeah, very interesting. But seriously, are your feet getting wet?"

"And did you also know," said Hilda, who didn't even realise Reggie was talking, "that around two thousand people die per year in lightning strikes? Singapore is a particularly dangerous location as it has the highest rate of lightning activity."

"Hilda," shouted Reggie. "Snap out of it and look down."

Hilda blinked. She didn't realise she had been chatting away about lightning for so long. "Sorry, Reggie. Not sure what happened. I think I was in some sort of trance." She looked down and saw that her feet and ankles were submerged in water. She looked up and saw water gushing out of a burst pipe. "Oh, well, that's not good."

"Tell me something I don't know."

"Okay," replied Hilda. "Did you know that a flash flood can reach over twenty feet high in a matter of minutes?"

"That's not what I meant."

"And did you know flash floods sweep away cars, flatten trees, collapse bridges, and even level buildings? They are the second most widespread natural disaster, after wildfires."

"Hilda, you're doing it again," said Reggie as he tried to wriggle out of the restraints.

"In fact, back in 1939, the Yangtze-Huai River Floods in China were responsible for the estimated death of around four million people. Many consider the flood to have been the deadliest natural disaster ever recorded in human history, unless you count Noah."

"You should definitely count Noah," replied Reggie, deciding his time was better served trying to get free from the restraints rather than trying to stop his friend from having a nervous breakdown. "Maybe you should tell me some facts about escape artists.

Preferably their methods of how they escaped."

"Certainty," replied Hilda, glad of the change of subject. "Most escape artists were extremely flexible and could bend their joints, allowing them to slip out of handcuffs and chains with relative ease."

"Great," replied Reggie as the water had now reached his knees. "So I've got roughly a minute to train my body to become double jointed. I might as well turn my arm

into a crowbar."

That was when Reggie suddenly felt loose and free to move. He easily slipped his right arm out of the restraints. Reggie scratched his head to work out what had just happened.

THUD

Something hard hit his head. He went to rub the lump with his hand.

THUD

It happened again.

Reggie looked at his arm.

"Oh, well, that is very unexpected."

"I know," replied Hilda. "And there were some escape artists who weren't as flexible that simple smuggled in a stanley knife and cut themselves free. Which is cheating, if you ask me."

Reggie had already pried the remaining restraints with his crowbar arm. "Well, needs must," replied Reggie as he carefully cut Hilda free using stanley knife that had appeared on the end of his left arm. "And if we were caught in a flash flood, what would be the safest way to escape?"

"Funny you should ask," said Hilda, who was on a roll. "66% of deaths occur when people try to either run away or drive out of the flood. The best course of action is to get as high as you can."

Reggie glanced around the basement and found the stairs. "Yes, that makes sense." He grabbed Hilda with one hand and hooked his arm under Mr Nitwhitt's armpit. He dragged them both towards the stairs as quickly as he could. The water was now over his belly button. He panicked as he realised they might not make it. "Got any facts on how to move through water quickly."

"Several," replied Hilda. "Human legs are very good on dry land, but completely useless underwater. Getting onto the surface is a much quicker way to travel across water. A rubber dinghy and a paddle are the best combination."

As she said that last sentence, Reggie felt his legs inflate. All three of them were suddenly sitting in a rubber dinghy that looked a bit like the trousers he was just wearing. Reggie looked at his left hand, which was still a stanley knife. "Did you say paddle?"

"Yes, a paddle."

"I thought so," replied Reggie as he watched his arm transform into a paddle. This was not the time to freak out, or ask questions, or call the family doctor and ask for as many crazy pills as he could fit in his mouth.

It was time to paddle.

Reggie pulled his arm through the water with all his strength. They easily reached the basement stairs in no time and glided upwards as the water level continued to rise.

"Did you know that a British naval officer called Peter Halkett invented the rubber dinghy? They were originally intended for Artic Explorers and could be used as a waterproof poncho before inflation."

"Fascinating," said Reggie. "I bet he never thought his invention would ever be used on a staircase." He found rowing quite enjoyable, unlike most eleven-year-old boys. So much so, he was now using two paddles, one on each arm. "Do go on."

"It's estimated that his invention has saved over a million lives. Dinghies are always used to carry people to safety after boats have capsized in open waters and to rescue people in flash floods."

"Well, I think we can make that a million and three lives now." Reggie gave one final push as they rowed up through the hatch and out of the school basement.

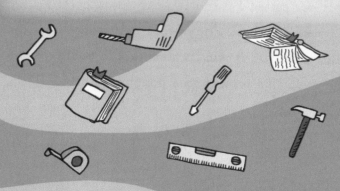

CHAPTER FIFTEEN
SUPERPOWERS

Reggie and Hilda collapsed to the ground in sheer relief.

The sun welcomed them back to the outside worlds with a cheeky fart (remember it is made of gas) and the wind kissed them on their cheeks (face cheeks, not bottom cheeks, the wind is much more polite than the big stinky gas ball in the sky).

The storm cloud that the caretaker's

PARDON ME!

weather machine laser had hit was nowhere to be seen. Nothing but clear skies for miles. Reggie touched his legs. They felt rubbery and a little inflated. On closer inspection, the left one seemed a bit larger than the other. He gave it a poke and it suddenly let out some air.

"Reggie," said Hilda. "Do you have my backpack?"

"Er," replied Reggie, as he was trying to make sense of what just happened. "No. I'm sorry Hilda."

"Oh, no." Hilda leapt to her feet and ran back to the basement hatch. "It must still be in the caretaker's basement. That flood has probably ruined all my encyclopaedias.

And your tool belt will be floating around somewhere too. We have to go back."

Reggie grabbed Hilda's arm to stop her. "I really don't think we need them anymore."

"What do you mean?"

"Don't you remember anything?" said Reggie. "Back in the basement. You keep on talking and talking and talking. I couldn't stop you."

"No," replied Hilda. "It's all a bit blurry. What was I talking about?"

Rather than answering her question, Reggie thought of a better idea. He always preferred the school lessons when the teacher didn't explain it in words but gave a demonstration.

WHAT'S THE LARGEST MAN-MADE STRUCTURE IN THE WORLD?

"The Great Wall of China," replied Hilda in under a second. "It's five-thousand-and-five-hundred miles long and took over two thousand years to build. Did you know the Chinese invented the wheelbarrow to help them build it quicker?"

HOW MANY ROOMS DOES THE WHITE HOUSE HAVE?

"One-hundred-and-thirty-two," replied Hilda in under half a second. "There are also four-hundred-and-twelve doors, one-hundred-and-forty-seven windows, thirty-five bathrooms, twenty-eight

fireplaces, eight staircases, and three elevators."

WHO INVENTED THE . . .

"Theodore H. Maiman," replied Hilda before Reggie could finish his question. "In 1960 at Hughes Research Laboratories, he built the first laser based on theoretical work by Charles Hard Townes and Arthur Leonard Schawlow. Laser is also an acronym that stands for *light amplification by stimulated emission of radiation*."

"And did you have to open a book to learn any of that random information?"

"Er," replied Hilda as she rubbed her head. It felt slightly warmer than the rest of her body and throbbed with knowledge.

"No. No, I didn't. I just instantly knew the answers." She then tried to think back to what happened and had a question of her own. "Did you just save us by transforming your arms into paddles and your legs into a rubber dinghy?"

Reggie wiggled his fingers in the air. They felt different. They looked like normal fingers, but he knew they were so much more than flesh and bone. "Yes. Yes, I did. You were saying what equipment we needed to escape, and *my body did the rest.*"

"Wow. That's incredible," said Hilda, staring at him. "I can hardly believe it. I'm a walking, talking encyclopaedia! It's like I've been hit over the head with a sledgehammer of knowledge."

Reggie went bright red as his right arm transformed into a sledgehammer. He gave it a strong wiggle, but it wouldn't change back. "Sorry, not sure how to make it stop."

Suddenly, Mr Nitwhitt sat up and screamed. Reggie panicked and whacked him on the head with his arm hammer. The

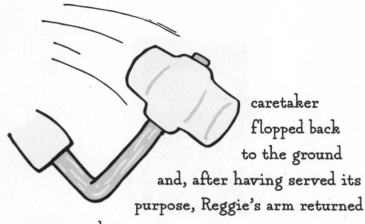

caretaker
flopped back
to the ground
and, after having served its
purpose, Reggie's arm returned
to normal.

"Well," said Hilda, "that answers that question."

The sound of high heels clip-clopped across the playground. Mrs Pudd, the headteacher, skidded around the corner. She looked at the kids, then are the flooded basement, and then at the caretaker.

"We're both fine, but he's unconscious," said Hilda. "I can put him in the recovery position, but I really don't think he deserves it."

Mrs Pudd's face turned a dark shade of

red. It was the kind of red that would make a raging bull question its own code of ethics and seek anger management counselling. The very round, very red women yelled at the top of her lungs.

CHAPTER SIXTEEN
HEADTEACHER

Reggie and Hilda sat silently in the headteacher's office.

They had explained everything to Mrs Pudd. How they trekked through a jungle and a snowstorm to deliver the parcels to the caretaker. How they discovered the weather machine and uncovered Mr Nitwhitt's plans

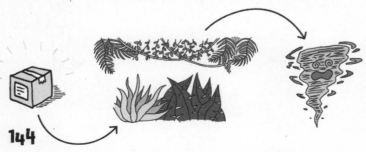

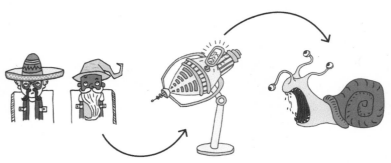

to create a super hurricane. How he captured them, strapped them to tables, pointed a giant laser at them and almost zapped them into dust particles. And, last but by no means least, how they were saved by a giant snail.

What they didn't include was the bit where all three of them were struck by green lightning and now had *superpowers*. That would make their story seem too farfetched. Plus, they didn't want anyone to know about that, not yet.

Mrs Pudd sat silently. She wore a boring brown three-piece suit with a matching handbag and high-heeled shoes. She only drank tea and only eat puddings. This meant

she was very round. In fact, she perfectly resembled a Cadbury's crème egg, which also happened to be her breakfast this morning.

She was the kind of woman perfectly suited to being a headteacher. When she was around parents and fellow teachers, she was as charming as a poodle on a good hair day. But when she was around her pupils, she was as horrible as a honey badger on VERY bad hair day, minus the honey. As you are about to find out.

said Mrs Pudd through gritted teeth.

Reggie and Hilda shot a confused eyebrow jiggle at each other. They'd never heard their headteacher say anything complimentary before. She usually just barked and shouted and said nasty things.

"Truly marvellous," continued the headmaster. "I'm especially grateful for your detailed explanation of the events, children. It will certainly help me decide how to punish the guilty party."

Something didn't add up. Reggie and Hilda could sense it in the atmosphere, like a spider patiently waiting for a fly to buzz into its web.

I REALLY MUST CONGRATULATE YOU BOTH . . .

. . . ON SETTING A NEW GUINNESS WORLD RECORD . . .

. . . FOR TELLING THE **MOST LIES** IN ONE STORY, YOU SNOT-FILLED, REVOLTING LITTLE **WORMS**

That's more like it.

Mrs Pudd stood up from behind her desk and looked down her nose at her victims. She had a scowl on her face that could melt Antarctica. She was the spider and Reggie and Hilda were the two juicy little flies trapped in her web. They strapped themselves in for a long headteacher rant.

"Weather machine, green lightning, super hurricane, silly hats, power crystals, giant lasers, evil supervillain? Utter nonsense! You've bunked off an entire afternoon of teaching. The school basement is flooded. The caretaker could be seriously hurt. And worse of all, you made me spill tea down my suit. Look, it's completely ruined."

ANTARCTICA
(AFTER MRS PUDD WENT FOR HER SUMMER HOLIDAYS)

148

TEA
(EARL GREY)

Reggie and Hilda tried to spot the stain but couldn't. Her suit was brown. It was one big tea-stain. There was a school rumour that Mrs Pudd had a bath in tea every single night and drank the bath water the next day. Otherwise, it would be a terrible waste.

She leaned in closer and barked even louder. "Do you think this institution is some sort of circus for your amusement? Do you believe that the laws of common sense do not apply within these walls? Do you think I won't shout at you until your ears fall off and your eyes dry out and your brains turn into mushy peas? Well, I've got news for you. I cannot and will not allow my repulsive pupils to make a mockery of me."

They glanced at each other. Reggie knew she could do all those things. Most kids who stumble out of the headteacher's office don't talk for an entire week. Hilda knew this rant was coming into land. And it was going to be a crash-landing right between their eyeballs.

"I need to know what actually happened. Right now. Or I'll have no choice but to

PERMANENTLY EXPEL

both of you . . .

¡IMMEDiATELY!

CHAPTER SEVENTEEN

EXPELLED

Reggie and Hilda were lost for words.

EXPELLED

PERMANENTLY

IMMEDIATELY

Hilda couldn't think of anything worse. Maybe losing her library card, but that can be replaced. Being excluded meant no more school. The thought of being home schooled by her parents was terrifying. Her dad was a Window Cleaner, and her mum was a Professional Online Quizzer. Her university dreams would be flushed down the toilet.

Reggie tried to look on the bright side. His parents had taught him there was always a silver lining. So, what was the upside of being excluded from school? Some kids might think he's cool. Perhaps he could build a nuclear reactor in the garage. He'd have all the nuclear power he'd ever need, but the shame of losing his education would live with him forever.

"So then," shouted the headteacher as she stared deep into their souls. "Who is going to tell me the truth?"

i WILL

They turned their heads to the door. In walked Mr Nitwhitt, with a bandage around his head.

"Boris, I'm so glad to see you've recovered. How do you feel?"

"A little shaken up," replied Mr Nitwhitt as he shut the door and joined Mrs Pudd next to her desk. "I have an enormous bruise on my head, but apart from that, I'm fine. Thanks for asking."

Reggie and Hilda looked at each other.

??? BORIS! ???

They even had an eyebrow wiggle for the exclamation mark, but this isn't the time to give you a lesson. What kind of supervillain has the name *Boris?* It made him seem like a . . . well, a middle-aged man who was a normal school caretaker.

"I thought it was best that you heard what happened this afternoon from me," said the caretaker, without looking at Reggie or Hilda. He firmly locked his eyes on the headteacher. "It should come from a trusted adult. I wouldn't want you believing anything but the truth."

All hope and happiness drained from Reggie and Hilda. Their futures dribbled down the chairs and soaked in the floor like melted ice cream. This was it. The caretaker had full control. Complete authority. Whatever he said next would seal their fate.

Mr Nitwhitt took and deep breath and said . . .

Well, that was unexpected. They couldn't believe what they heard. And it was about to get even more unexpected.

"I was fixing a leaky pipe in the basement when it suddenly burst in my face. Before I could stand again, knee-high water filled the basement. I panicked. I love a bath, but apart from that, water is my worse fear. I can't swim. These two children must have been playing near the hatch and heard my cry for help. They somehow broke in, bravely swam into the torrent of water, and pulled me out. Without them, I'd be a goner."

Everyone was speechless. You could hear a pin drop in the pin dropping factory next

door. Even Reggie and Hilda's eyebrows
froze in place from utter shock.

"Well, headteacher," said the caretaker,
breaking the silence. "Aren't you going to
say anything? There are two little heroes
in your school who deserve to be praised for
their act of bravery."

Mrs Pudd shook her
head. Her cheeks
wobbled as though two
lumps of jelly were stuck
to her face. "Certainly
not," she replied with
disdain. "Don't forget
they have damaged school property ... "

THE PRESTIGIOUS SCHOOL
AWARD FOR ACTS OF INCREDIBLE
BRAVERY

"To save my life, Mrs Pudd," said Mr
Nitwhitt, finishing her sentence for her.

She grunted, then throw a pencil across

the room. She threw it with such
force it stuck in the wall like an arrow.
"Bother! I was really looking forward to
expelling these rotten little maggots. I
haven't done that in ages."

She looked at the kids and said in a slow,
serious voice. "You may leave. But remember
this. I'm watching you. One tiny slip and
I'll have you both back in here quicker
than a rocket-fuelled hamster wearing
rollerblades. Now get out."

Reggie and Hilda slid off the chairs and
scuttled to the door. They had enough time
to glance back at the caretaker and spot a
glint in his eye.

And it wasn't one of those nice little
innocent glints you see in a film.

It was an **EVIL GLINT**.

CHAPTER EIGHTEEN
SUPER NERDS

What a wonderful noise. Much better than the evil laugh of a super villain or a snail's deafening roar. The ringing of the school bell was an even better sound than normal, especially for the two students who had saved it. It rang out its thanks across the school as the pupils of Churchill Junior School ran out of their classrooms as quick as lickety-split.

Reggie and Hilda also ran, but not for the playground like everyone else. They were heading for their favourite bench at the front of the school to do what they always did at lunchtime. Only now the pair had less to carry.

WHAT'S A METAMORPHIC ROCK?

asked Reggie,
as he fiddled with his dad's old Game Boy Advance in one hand and held his cheese and ham sandwich in the other. If you looked closely, you would discover that each of his fingers had transformed into tiny tools like

a fleshy Swiss-army knife.

Hilda resisted the muscle memory, telling her to open her backpack. She thumbed through her brain until she found the information she needed and took a bite of her chicken and bacon sandwich. "Metamorphic rocks form through a process called metamorphism. The original rock is exposed to temperatures greater than 200 degrees and pressure of 100 mega pascals, causing it to recrystallize into a new mineral composition."

The girl adjusted her glasses, surprising even herself at how clever she sounded, and continued to channel her encyclopaedic memory. "Examples of metamorphic rocks include gneiss, slate, marble, schist, and quartzite. My particular favourite is marble, which the Greeks called 'shining stone' and covers the entire Taj Mahal."

"I love your follow-up facts, Hilda."

"Thanks, Reggie. But you better make that the last question." Hilda rubbed her head and said, "I don't want to get another one of those headaches. The last time I overused my new superpowers, it felt like someone had hit me over the head with a sledgehammer."

SLAM!

"Oh, whoops! Sorry."

Reggie looked at the Game Boy Advance. Not much was left. It covered the playground like plastic confetti. He picked himself up

off the floor, but didn't have the strength to lift his left arm. "Great, thanks Hilda. Now my hand is a sledgehammer. How am I going to hide this when I go back into class?"

Hilda smiled. It was still very odd to look at her friend and not see his trusty tool belt wrapped around his waist.

"I'm not sure, but if anyone can work it out, *The Handy Man* can."

Reggie rolled his eyes. "Now that I hear it out loud, I don't like my superhero name. Who wants to be saved by a handyman? Can I change it?"

"Sure," replied Hilda. "I was thinking of changing mine, too."

"But I like *Wiki Girl*."

"Yeah, but I'm pretty sure I can't use a trademarked name like Wikipedia. That's the kind of thing that earns you a lawsuit," said the author, I mean Hilda.

"Well, we've got plenty of time to think of the perfect names." Reggie pulled himself back onto the bench and said, "Pliers." His arm changed into the much lighter tool that he then used to pick a piece of gravel from his sandwich. "Maybe we should reconsider Mr Nitwhitt's supervillain name, too."

Hilda wiggled her eyebrows in protest.

"What?! But I thought we are going to call him *Mr Slime.*"

"I just think that we shouldn't assume that slime is his superpower," replied Reggie. "What if the next time we see him he has his very own Snail Army of Doom?"

"You and the snail army of doom. You just can't let it go, can you?!"

"Nope," replied Reggie, not even caring how ridiculously silly it sounded.

Hilda crossed her arms and said, "We still can't be sure that he really is a super villain. Not after what happened in the headteachers office. He might have changed his ways."

"I suppose so," replied Reggie reluctantly.

MR SLIME

"So, it's back to the drawing board for all the names, then. Oh, come on!" He looked down at his torso to see his chest and stomach had transformed into a chalkboard with all his fingers were different coloured chalks.

Hilda laughed. "I think we've got bigger problems than what our superhero names are. Anyway, we know exactly what we are calling our superhero team, right?"

"Right," replied Reggie with a smile. "*The Super Nerds* have arrived and are here to protect the school." He looked at himself one more time, then added, "and write down your grocery list."

EPILOGUE

A figure lurked in the darkness.

It was silent and still. It cast a shadow as black as the deepest depths of the universe. It oozed evil like an octopus with a particularly nasty cold and a leaky ink glans. Oh yeah, and it smelt pretty bad too.

The figure was alone, sitting on an empty crate behind the school. He seemed to be talking to himself, which was not an unusual thing to do. But the subject matter was disturbing and, every now and then, the ground seemed to move.

"Settle down, my slimy friends," said the figure to the ground. "We'll soon have our opportunity to strike back. You know the plan. Beautifully simple, and yet astonishingly brilliant."

The figure drummed his long fingers together in pleasure. He showed his yellowed teeth as he grinned to himself. "I know, I know. I truly am a marvellous supervillain. And you should all be proud to be my tiny minions. You magnificent creatures. I am nothing without *my Snail Army of Doom*."

The flattery seemed to make the ground blush. It moved around in a contented kind

of way. The figure stood up and paced back and forth. "You are still wondering why I saved those children, aren't you? Well, now that I am a supervillain, with my very own superpower, I've realised something. Destroying Churchill Junior School won't be much fun without having a nemesis to watch it with me in delightful despair." He turned to the ground and added, "it's not greedy to have two nemeses, is it?"

The ground didn't reply but, none the less, the figure answered it. "Good. I hate those two pathetic children. A master plan that didn't involve destroying them is simply unthinkable." He carried on pacing, avoiding the tiny creatures on the ground, and added, "still, I know I am outnumbered. But not for long. For out of my unexpected

accident, a wonderful creation was born. The supernatural lightning cloud is somewhere, waiting to find its next lucky victim to strike. And when it does, I'll be ready to employ a new trainee villain."

Lightning crackled in the distance. The sky flashed a nuclear green and was quickly followed by a roll of thunder.

"Let the recruitment drive begin."

WANT TO FIND OUT
WHAT HAPPENS NEXT?

READ EPISODE TWO TO
FIND OUT NOW!

WARNING:
THIS BOOK CONTAINS OVER 20
GROSS SNEEZES AND A SNAIL
WITH NO EYEBALLS

IT'S COMPETITION TIME

THE GREEN SUPERNATURAL CLOUD
IS ZAPPING KIDS AND GIVING THEM
SUPER POWERS!

IMAGINE IF YOU WERE NEXT . . . WHAT SUPER POWERS
WOULD YOU HAVE? WHAT WOULD YOUR COSTUME LOOK LIKE?
WHAT WOULD YOUR SUPERHERO NAME BE?

THE AMAZING SPAGHETTI BOY

HIS ENEMY
MEATBALL MAN

EACH MONTH A NEW WINNER WILL RECIEVE A SIGNED
BOOK (YOU CAN CHOOSE WHICH ONE). REMEMBER TO INCLUDE
YOUR NAME AND THE DRAWING AS AN ATTACHMENT.

EMAIL YOUR DRAWING TO ENTER THE COMPETITION:

ME@CJWARWOOD.COM

ONE ENTRY PER CHILD.
GOOD LUCK!

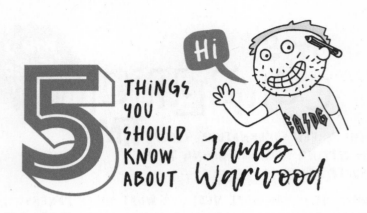

5 THINGS YOU SHOULD KNOW ABOUT James Warwood

Hi

1 THE BEST THING ABOUT BEING AN AUTHOR IS THE OPPORTUNITY TO INSPIRE KIDS TO BE CREATIVE WITH WORDS AND DOODLES
(BUT THAT'S A MASSIVE FIB, BECAUSE THE GENUINE ANSWER IS BELOW)

It's the most common question I get when visiting schools — what's the best thing about being an author?

I always have to lie, because there are adults in the room that would judge me and become insanely jealous. Well, I'm finally ready to reveal the world exclusive real answer — the best thing about being an author is . . . you can have a bath at any time of the day!

Soaking in a lovely warm bath with loads of bubbles and a tasty snack is my happy place. And I don't have an annoying boss who says I can't do that at 10am.

In fact, I'm writing this in the bath right now!

THE BEST THING ABOUT BEING AN AUTHOR

 WHEN i WAS A YOUNG LAD, i TOLD EVERYONE TO STOP CALLING ME JAMES AND START CALLING ME JAZZ

I was around ten years old. I was watching a TV show called 'The Fresh Prince of Bel Air'.

In walks a character with THE BEST name my young ears had ever heard — Jazz. He was cool. He was musical. He was friends with Will Smith. All the things that I wanted to be.

And his acual name was even better — DJ Jazzy Jeff.

I thought to myself, *I don't have a nickname yet, and the first two letters are the same as my name, so it's a no-brainer.*

I told my dad that, from now on, he was to call me by the name Jazz. He laughed. Then I told my older sister. She laughed too. I don't remember what my mum's reaction was, but she is much nicer, so she probably smiled

encouragingly while she laughed in her head.
Anyway, the nickname only lasted a week.

 **i WROTE THiS BOOK WHiLST iN HiDiNG FROM MY WiFE AND 2ND NEWBORN SON**

On 10th December 2021, we had our second child.

Now, I'm sure I don't need to tell you this, but adults are stupid. Here's a good example. Most parents assume that, because they've kept their first baby alive, that the next one is going to be super easy. A walk in the park. No problem at all. But they soon realise how wrong they were when their newborn baby has vomited everywhere, and their toddler

TIME FOR A SHOWER.
THANKS, LIL BRO

rolls
around
in it like a hippo.

As an escape from the
chaos, I wrote something fun and silly and
stupid. I would sneak out of the house and
hid in coffee shops with my laptop. I wrote
this book in one month.

I then completely forgot about it. Two years
later, I found it and published it.

4 MY FAVOURITE BOOK IS TREASURE ISLAND BY ROBERT LOUIS STEVENSON

There are so many great things about this
book. Pirates. Doubloons. Gun fights. A

treasure map. Parrots.

But the best thing is that, whenever I read this book, I have flashbacks to watching 'Muppets Treasure Island', which is also based on the book. The combination of the book and the film floating around my head is fantastic.

And one of the best things about having kids is getting to share this stuff with them. My eldest loves watching the film (and we always have a sword fight during the end scene, because we are true fans).

And now I'm currently reading a kid's version of the book to him and we're both loving it!

Aren't books amazing!

5   I'M DYSLEXIC, BUT I THINK THAT'S ACTUALLY A GOOD THING

Do you think that's weird?

An author who is dyslexic, and happy?

Yep, I suppose it is a little weird, but that's the secret to a happy life — discover who you are, and then learn to live with it.

For a long time, I told myself that reading and writing were not me. I'm slow at both things. I struggle with spellings. I reread the same page a lot, because I forget where I am.

But I LOVE stories. I'm constantly daydreaming, my imagination running wild inside my head, thinking up silly stories and funny characters and crazy adventures. That's my dyslexic brain being super creative.

So, I've worked hard to bring those stories to life — with the help of cool software and human helpers and sheer willpower. Because this is what I enjoy doing, writing books and then doodling in them.

And my dyslexia has become a part of the process.

OTHER BOOKS BY JAMES WARWOOD

THE SUPER NERDS

Epidose Two: The Golden Sneeze Machine

MIDDLE-GRADE STAND-ALONE FICTION

The Chef Who Cooked Up a Catastrophe
The Boy Who Stole One Million Socks

The Girl Who Vanquished the Dragon

TRUTH OR POOP?

True or false quiz books.

Learn something new and laugh as you do it!

Book One: Amazing Animals
Book Two: Spectacular Space
Book Three: Gloriously Gross
Book Four: Incredible Insects
Book Five: Dangerous Dinosaurs
Book Six: Puzzling Predators

THE 49 SERIES

Non-fiction cartoon series full of helpful tips and laugh-out-loud silliness for getting the most out of life.

49 Excuses for Not Tidying Your Bedroom
49 Ways to Steal the Cookie Jar
49 Excuses for Not Doing Your Homework
49 Questions to Annoy Your Parents
49 Excuses for Skipping Gym Class
49 Excuses for Staying Up Past Your Bedtime
49 Excuses for Being Really Really Late
49 Excuses for Not Eating Your Vegetables
49 Excuses for Not Doing Your Chores
49 Excuses for Getting the Most Out of Christmas
49 Excuses for Extending Your Summer Holiday
49 Excuses for Bagging More Candy at Halloween

WHERE TO FIND JAMES ONLINE

ORDER BOOKS DIRECT FROM THE AUTHOR

Website:
www.cjwarwood.com
Facebook & Instagram:
search for James
Warwood